Charles Colcock Jones

The Life and Services of the Honorable Maj. Gen Samuel

Elbert

Charles Colcock Jones

The Life and Services of the Honorable Maj. Gen Samuel Elbert

ISBN/EAN: 9783337056292

Printed in Europe, USA, Canada, Australia, Japan

Cover: Foto ©Raphael Reischuk / pixelio.de

More available books at **www.hansebooks.com**

THE LIFE AND SERVICES

OF THE

HONORABLE

MAJ. GEN. SAMUEL ELBERT

OF GEORGIA

CHARLES C. JONES, JR., LL. D.

An Address *delivered before* The Georgia Historical Society, *at Savannah, on the 6th of December, 1886*

PRINTED FOR THE SOCIETY

The Riverside Press, Cambridge
MDCCCLXXXVII

MAJOR–GENERAL SAMUEL ELBERT.

MR. PRESIDENT, LADIES, AND GENTLEMEN :

Responding to the flattering invitation extended by the Lecture Committee of this Society, I come to-night, my friends, to recall the image of one who, a century ago, was the honored chief magistrate of this commonwealth, — who acted a conspicuous part in our colonial struggle for independence, — who was numbered among the earliest and the most zealous " Sons of Liberty," — whose reputation, both civil and military, was free from all alloy, — who bore himself on every occasion as a courageous man and a worthy citizen, — who sleeps in an unmarked grave within cannon-range of this Hall in which we are now assembled to render tribute to his virtues, — and of whom, so far as our information extends, we possess no portrait save such as his own brave hand has painted on the historic canvas.

To the Continental Army Georgia furnished only two officers who attained the rank of Brig-

adier-General. They were Lachlan McIntosh
and Samuel Elbert. Both were excellent soldiers, sterling patriots, and influential citizens.
Their services alike in peace and in war were
held in high repute. It is of the latter of them
that we would speak.

Born in the province of South Carolina seven
years after Oglethorpe had planted his colony
upon Yamacraw Bluff, and of English parent-
age, his youth was spent in the Parish of Prince
William, where his father, a Baptist clergyman,
had charge of a congregation. Of the early life
of Samuel Elbert but little is known. While
still a lad he was deprived by death of both his
parents. In quest of employment he repaired to
Savannah, in Georgia, where his steady habits,
energy, honesty, and upright conduct soon com-
mended him to general favor. There, entering
upon a commercial life, by his integrity and de-
votion to business he won the confidence and
secured preferment at the hands of those with
whom he was associated. For several years an-
tecedent to the outbreak of the Revolutionary
War he was recognized as a leading and prosperous merchant in the commercial metropolis of
the province. With the Indians his trade rela-
tions were extensive. His marriage with Miss
Elizabeth Rae confirmed his social position and
influence. While still a young man he manifested a decided taste for military affairs ; and,

during the latter years of Governor Wright's administration, held a captain's commission in a company of Grenadiers.

Savannah was then the capital of Georgia, and the home of considerable wealth and refinement. The only town which aspired to a rivalry with it for the trade of the colony was Sunbury, situated near the mouth of Midway River. When the disagreements between England and her American colonies became serious, and public sentiment was divided, Captain Elbert promptly enrolled himself among the " Sons of Liberty." Of the Council of Safety which convened on the 22d of June, 1775, and was composed of such influential patriots as Noble W. Jones, Archibald Bulloch, John Houstoun, William Ewen, Joseph Clay, Edward Telfair, George Walton, and Joseph Habersham, he was an efficient member. By the action of this body was Georgia placed in correspondence with the Continental Congress and with the Councils of Safety of the other revolting provinces. Then was a union flag defiantly hoisted upon a liberty pole. Then were thirteen patriotic toasts proposed, and responded to by salutes from two field-pieces and by martial music. Then were resolutions adopted pledging Georgia to the common cause of American liberty.

To the Provincial Congress, which assembled in Savannah on the 4th of July in the same year, Captain Elbert was a delegate. This was Georgia's first secession convention. It committed the province to positive sympathy and confederated alliance with the twelve sister American colonies; — practically annulled within her limits the operation of the objectionable acts of Parliament; — questioned the supremacy of British rule, and inaugurated measures intended to accomplish the independence of the plantation and its erection into the dignity of a State. By that Congress was Samuel Elbert chosen a member of the Council of Safety charged with the conduct of public affairs and empowered to provide for the common defense. The organization of the militia enlisted the liveliest interest, and the most potent measures at command were adopted by this Council to enroll, officer, and equip the arms-bearing population of, the province.[1] All vessels which would engage to import war materials were declared exempt from the penalties of the non-importation agreement, and Samuel Elbert, Edward Telfair, and Joseph Habersham were appointed a committee to supply Georgia with arms and ammunition. They were authorized to contract for the purchase of four hundred muskets with bayonets, twenty

---

[1] A committee, consisting of Stephen Drayton, Samuel Elbert, Dr. Nathan Brownson, and Peter Tarlin, was raised and commissioned to prepare a report upon the militia of the province, with such suggestions as might be deemed proper for its efficient organization.

thousand pounds of gunpowder, and sixty thousand pounds of cannon-balls, bullets, bar-lead, grape and swan shot. The battalion raised under the resolution of the Continental Congress for the protection of Georgia was organized on the 7th of January, 1776, by the enrollment of eight companies, fully officered, and by the appointment of Lachlan McIntosh as Colonel, Samuel Elbert as Lieutenant-Colonel, and Joseph Habersham as Major. From this time until the conclusion of the Revolutionary War Colonel Elbert was actively engaged in the military service of the struggling confederacy.

On the 19th of May, 1776, Major Joseph Habersham married Miss Isabella Rae, — a sister-in-law of Colonel Elbert. This cemented a friendship already existing between that officer and Major Habersham's younger brother, — Lieutenant John Habersham, — who was soon announced as Brigade Major of the Georgia forces upon the Continental establishment. During their joint service in Georgia these officers were at all times associated upon terms of the closest intimacy, and together shared the common peril.

The first passage at arms in Georgia between the King's soldiers and the rebels occurred at Savannah, early in March, 1776. Only a little while before, Governor Wright, escaping from confinement, sought and found refuge on board the armed ship Scarborough, — Captain Barclay, — lying in Tybee roadstead. Influenced by the representations of the fugitive governor, and anxious to procure supplies for their troops, Captain Barclay and Major Grant resolved to obtain by force what their negotiations had failed to secure. Many vessels laden with rice were then at anchor near the Savannah wharves and along the opposite side of the river. So unsettled was the political situation that they were forbidden by the Council of Safety to proceed to sea. Purposing the capture of these vessels and their cargoes, Captain Barclay — attended by his fleet, and accompanied by Majors Maitland and Grant in command of between two and three hundred light infantry and marines conveyed in two transport ships — ascended the Savannah River and actually took possession of some of them. Without recounting the details of the affair, suffice it to say that the designs of the enemy were thwarted mainly through the vigilance of Colonel McIntosh, supported by Lieutenant-Colonel Elbert and Major Habersham. In obedience to orders issued by the Council of Safety, many of these rice-laden vessels were burnt, and the enemy was kept at bay by a battery of three 4-pounder guns planted on Yamacraw Bluff and by a force of three hundred men there embodied.

St. Augustine, — the chief town of Florida, — with its garrison of British troops, Indians, and Loyalists, was a thorn in the side of Georgia. Thence were projected marauding parties which, time and again, invaded the southern portions of the province, robbing and murdering the inhabitants. After the successful defense of the fort on Sullivan's Island, General Charles Lee conceived the idea of subjugating East Florida. To that end he ordered a concentration of the forces of South Carolina and Georgia. Their advance, however, was countermanded at Sunbury.

Colonel Lachlan McIntosh's promotion to the grade of Brigadier-General and his assignment to the command of all the Georgia troops serving on the Continental establishment, gave great offense to Button Gwinnett who had been an avowed candidate for that position. Elected on the 4th of March, 1777, by the Council of Safety, President and Commander-in-Chief of Georgia, to serve as such until a governor could be regularly chosen in accordance with constitutional provisions, he determined to signalize his administration by an expedition against St. Augustine. The project was pleasing to the public, and an ambitious desire to overrun East Florida and annex it to Georgia took firm possession of the breast of the acting governor. Instead of entrusting the command of this ex-

pedition to General McIntosh, who, as the rank-
ing military officer of the forces present for the
protection of Georgia, was in all fairness and in
accordance with established usage entitled to ex-
pect and to claim it, Gwinnett, wishing to mortify
his successful competitor for the honor of which
we have spoken, and manifestly intending to
heap an affront upon him, publicly announced
that he would in person direct the army of occupation.   General McIntosh was not permitted
even to accompany the expedition.   Saw-pit Bluff
— twelve miles from the mouth of the river St.
John — was designated as the place, and the
12th of May as the time, for the rendezvous of
the forces which were to participate in the contemplated subjugation of East Florida.   Colonel
Baker, with the Georgia militia, was directed to
march by land, while Colonel Elbert was ordered
to conduct the Continental troops by water to
the point indicated.   Near Nassau River the
former officer was met and routed by Colonels
Brown and McGirth.   Colonel Elbert was sore
perplexed upon finding that he was placed in
command of the Continental forces detailed for
this expedition, to the exclusion of General Mc-
Intosh, who, as his superior officer, was entitled
to that distinction.   He was also concerned at
the abnormal situation consequent upon orders
promulgated by President Gwinnett, by which
he was required to report directly to and receive

his instructions from the President and Council. On the 24th of April he addressed an official communication [1] to General McIntosh, advising him of the disagreeable and unsatisfactory plight in which he found himself, and expressing his regrets that his orders did not come through his commanding general. He even ventured to call the attention of the President and Council to this irregularity. Gwinnett, however, controlled that body : and, being of an imperious will and implacable in his hate, continued to supplant General McIntosh and to subject him to at least apparent humiliation.

Having advanced as far south as the north end of Amelia Island, — having there been informed of the defeat of Colonel Baker, — finding the enemy in force and on the alert, — perceiving that a hot sun and exposure were causing much sickness in his command, — well knowing that his provisions were being rapidly consumed, and seeing small prospect of forcing the coast-guard and obtaining a fresh supply from the country adjacent to the mouth of the St. John, — and advised that war-vessels were standing on and off waiting to intercept his galleys should they attempt to approach the point of rendez-vous, Colonel Elbert wisely resolved to give over his purpose and retire to Frederica. Thence he returned to Savannah. Thus ended an ex-

[1] See MS. Order Book of Colonel Elbert.

pedition conceived in ambition and jealousy, planned without due consideration, marred in its execution, and utterly without benefit in its results.

Gwinnett was a candidate for the office of Governor of Georgia. John Adam Treutlen opposed him, and was elected by a handsome majority. McIntosh was numbered among his ardent supporters. He did not hesitate openly to avow his gratification at Treutlen's success. In fact, he publicly denounced Gwinnett in unmeasured terms. The quarrel between these gentlemen culminated on the 15th of May, when Gwinnett challenged McIntosh to mortal combat. They met the next morning at sunrise within the present limits of the city of Savannah. Pistol shots were exchanged at the short distance of twelve feet. Both were wounded in the thigh, — McIntosh dangerously, Gwinnett fatally. The former was confined to his couch for some time, and the latter, after lingering for twelve days, died of his hurt. So intense was the excitement caused by this duel and the death of Gwinnett that General McIntosh, after indictment, trial, and acquittal, acting under the advice of friends, left Georgia for a season. Repairing to the headquarters of General Washington, he was by him assigned to duty in the western districts of Virginia and Pennsylvania.

Upon the departure of General McIntosh

Colonel Elbert succeeded to the command of
the Continental forces in Georgia. His headquarters were at Savannah, although he was fre-
quently on the southern frontier of the State
which was harassed by incursions of the enemy
issuing from Florida. Recruiting officers ex-
perienced much difficulty in filling the ranks of
companies attached to the battalions authorized
by Congress. The bounty and pay allowed by
the general government for a year's service did
not equal the sum offered by a militiaman for
a substitute to take his place for only three
months. Many, disposed to enter the army, pre-
ferred enlistment for a short term with the militia, where they could act pretty much as they
pleased and remain near their homes, to being
mustered into the regular service for a period of
three years, when they would be subjected to
strict discipline and find themselves liable to
duty in distant fields. The paper currency, too,
which at first was accepted at par in defrayal of
all expenses, was now rapidly depreciating in
value.

In April, 1778, General Robert Howe, then
in command of the Southern Department and
having his headquarters at Savannah, was informed that General Prevost was about to set
out from Florida to invade Georgia. To repel
this anticipated incursion, and thereafter to move
forward for the subjugation of East Florida,

Governor Houstoun and General Howe resolved upon the immediate mobilization of the military strength of the State. Of the Georgia militia the governor proposed to take personal command. When summoned to the field they did not aggregate more than three hundred and fifty men, and many of them were poorly armed and badly disciplined. The Continental forces within the limits of the State, numbering about five hundred and fifty, were to be led by Colonel Elbert. They were to be supplemented by two hundred and fifty Continental infantrymen, and thirty artillerists with two field-pieces, drawn from South Carolina and commanded by Colonel Charles Cotesworth Pinckney. The Carolina militia, under Colonels Bull and Williamson, were ordered to rendezvous at Purrysburg, on the Savannah River. Fort Howe, on the Alatamaha, was selected as the place of concentration.

On the 14th of April Colonel Elbert reached that point with his command. The next day, learning that several of the enemy's vessels were lying at and near Frederica, he detailed three hundred men, exclusive of officers, with fifty rounds of ammunition and six days' rations apiece, and with no baggage except their blankets, and a detachment of artillerists with two field-pieces, to proceed to Darien, and there, going on board the galleys, to advance to Pike's

Bluff, distant rather more than a mile from Frederica.[1] This expedition the colonel conducted in person. What subsequently transpired may best be told in the language of Colonel Elbert, who, in a letter to General Howe, communicated the following interesting details of a gallant exploit : —

"FREDERICA, *April 19th*, 1778.

" DEAR GENERAL, — I have the happiness to inform you, that about 10 o'clock this forenoon the brigantine Hinchinbrooke, the sloop Rebecca, and a prize brig, all struck the British tyrant's colors and surrendered to the American arms.

" Having received intelligence that the above vessels were at this place, I put about three hundred men, by detachment from the troops under my command at Fort Howe, on board the three galleys, — the Washington, Captain Hardy, — the Lee, Captain Braddock, — and the Bulloch, Captain Hatcher; — and a detachment of artil-

---

[1] The following is the order of detail : —

"HEAD QUARTERS FORT HOWE.
15*th April*, 1778.

"A Detachment of three Field Officers, 6 Captains, Eighteen Subalterns, twenty four Sergt', two Fifers, 6 Drummers, and Three Hundred rank and file by Detail from the line, also a Detachment of Artillery with two field pieces, to be in readiness to march early tomorrow ; — each man with 50 rounds of Ammunition and 6 Days Provisions. This Party are to carry no Baggage except Blankets.

"By order of the Colonel Commanding
JOHN HABERSHAM, *Brigade Major.*"
See MS. Order Book of Colonel Elbert.

2

lery with two field-pieces, under Captain Young, I put on board a boat. With this little army we embarked at Darien, and last evening effected a landing at a bluff about a mile below the town, leaving Colonel White on board the Lee, Captain Melvin on board the Washington, and Lieutenant Petty on board the Bulloch, each with a sufficient party of troops. Immediately on landing I dispatched Lieutenant-Colonel Rae and Major Roberts, with about one hundred men, who marched directly up to the town and made prisoners three marines and two sailors belonging to the Hinchinbrooke.

"It being late, the galleys did not engage until this morning. You must imagine what my feelings were to see our three little men-of-war going on to the attack of these three vessels who have spread terror on our coast, and who were drawn up in order of battle : but the weight of our metal soon damped the courage of these heroes, who soon took to their boats, and, as many as could, abandoned the vessels with everything on board, of which we immediately took possession. What is extraordinary, we have not one man hurt. Captain Ellis, of the Hinchinbrooke, is drowned, and Captain Mowbray, of the Rebecca, made his escape. As soon as I see Colonel White, who has not yet come to us with his prizes,[1] I shall consult with him, the three

[1] These prizes, by direction of Colonel Elbert, were conducted

other officers, and the commanding officers of the galleys, on the expediency of attacking the Galatea, now lying at Jekyll."

Seeing the preparations made for her capture, the Galatea took counsel of her fears and departed. This gallant exploit inspired the troops, and was hailed by General Howe as a good omen of the success which he believed would crown his demonstration against Florida.[1] The stores acquired with these vessels were most opportune.

Informed of the presence of the American forces at Fort Howe, General Prevost paused in his movement, and busied himself with repairing his defensive works on the rivers St. Mary and St. John, with mounting guns at Fort Tonyn, and with maturing plans for the protection of East Florida. Neither at St. Mary nor at Fort Tonyn, however, did General Howe encounter

to Sunbury for safe-keeping, and were there placed in charge of Major John Jones.

See MS. Order Book of Colonel Elbert.

[1] On the 13th of May, 1778, at Fort Howe, General Howe published the following complimentary order : —

"The General thinks proper to express in public orders how highly he approves the conduct of Colonel Elbert in the late Expedition against the Enemy at Frederica, and with equal pleasure applauds the spirited behaviour of the Officers and Men both of the Galleys and of the Army who were upon that Command. This he would certainly have done earlier, but his absence from the Army, and the hurry he has been in since his arrival, deprived him until now of that satisfaction."

See MS. Order Book of Colonel Elbert.

any serious resistance from the enemy. Prevost
prudently withdrew his forces from his advanced
posts, and covered the approaches to St. Augustine. From their position on Alligator Creek
Colonel Clarke gallantly but vainly attempted
the dislodgment of the English regulars and
Loyalists. It was evidently the intention of the
British general to offer no determined opposition
until he had enticed the Americans as far as the
river St. John.[1] There he hoped to turn upon
them and inflict severe loss, if not utter anni-
hilation. Howe's command was by this time in
a wretched and despondent plight. A malarial
region, intense heat, bad water, insufficient shel-

---

[1] Lieutenant-Colonel Joseph Habersham, who was then serving
with Colonel Elbert, writing from the "Camp on the South side
of Satilla River," under date "17th June, 1778," says: "We
are now, a part of us, on the south side of Satilla, within 15
miles of Fort Tonyn. . . . Genl Howe with the Carolina Brigade will be here this evening, and the Governor with the Militia
was on last Tuesday at Read's Bluff, so that I hope we shall
very shortly be able to give a good account of Col Brown and
his Scout, unless he should prudently make his escape to his
good Friends the Red Coats, who, I fancy, will hardly risk a
Battle on this side of St. Johns. . . . Colonel Elbert is hearty.
He frets a little on account of Howe's and the Governor's tar-
diness."

From Fort Tonyn, on the 5th of July, 1778, he writes: "The
Governor and the Militia are to join us to-day. I hope the Captain and Major General will lay their heads together so that we
may go on or return, for I am tired of staying here."

To the courtesy of William Neyle Habersham, Esqr., of Savannah, am I indebted for access to the original letters from
which the above extracts are made.

ter, and salt meat so impaired the health of his troops that the hospital returns showed one half the men upon the sick-list. Many had been left at Fort Howe, incapacitated by disease. Through lack of forage thirty-five horses had perished, and those which remained were so enfeebled that they were incapable of transporting the cannon, ammunition, provisions, and baggage of the army. The soldiers were in large measure dispirited and distracted. The command was rent by factions, and there was no leading spirit to mould its discordant elements into a harmonious and an efficient whole. Governor Houstoun, remembering the powers conferred by his executive council, refused, with his militia, to receive orders from General Howe. Colonel Williamson's troops would not yield obedience to a Continental officer, and Commodore, Bowen insisted that the naval forces were distinct from and independent of the land service. Thus was the general compelled to rely mainly upon the Continental troops of Colonels Elbert and Pinckney. Had a masterly mind been present, quickly would these ridiculous and unpatriotic factions have been consolidated; rapidly, by stern orders and enforced obedience, would the army in all its parts have been unified and brought into efficient subjection. But there was no potent voice to evoke order out of confusion, — no iron will to dominate over the emergency. General

Howe simply accepted the situation as he found it, and, discouraged by perplexing delays, appalled by the sickness of the troops, embarrassed by the want of coöperation among subordinates, the lack of stores, and the inefficiency of the transportation department, and uncertain as to the future, convened a council of war at Fort Tonyn on the 11th of July, to pass upon the expediency, if not the necessity, of abandoning the expedition. That council having resolved that its further prosecution was impracticable, the troops were, on the 14th of July, 1778, ordered to return to their former stations.[1]

[1] The following is the order published by General Howe upon the termination of the campaign :—

"CAMP AT FORT TONYN, 14th July, 1778.

" *Parole, Savannah.*

"The General leaves the Army to day. He parts with it with reluctance and from no other motive than to make those provisions at proper places necessary to its accommodation. He embraces this opportunity to testify how highly he approves the Conduct both of Officers and Men whom he had the honour to command. The readiness with which the Officers received orders, and the punctuality with which they executed them, gave pleasure to the General, and did honour to themselves. The cheerfulness with which the Men supported a long and fatiguing march under a variety of unavoidable yet distressing circumstances, gives them an undoubted claim to the characters of Good Soldiers, and is a happy presage of the service they will in future render to the Glorious Cause in which they are engaged. Commandants of Brigades will take care that this order be made known both to Officers and Men.

" N. EVELEIGH, Col: & D. A. G."

See MS. Order Book of Colonel Elbert.

The above order was evidently intended for the troops serv-

Thus, for the third time, was the hope of the re-
duction of St. Augustine and the dispersion of
the British forces in East Florida relinquished.
The most that can be said in favor of this campaign, with its lamentable lack of preparation,
want of management, disagreement between com-
manders, surprising mistakes, inexcusable delays,
vexatious disappointments, and fruitless expenditure of men and munitions, is that it retarded
the inroads of the enemy. This suspension of
hostilities, however, was of short duration.

In the fall of 1778, Lord George Germain resolved to transfer the theatre of active warfare
from the Northern to the Southern provinces.
His hopes were fixed upon the early conquest of
Georgia and South Carolina. For the accom-
plishment of this purpose General Augustine
Prevost — then in command of East Florida —
was instructed to invade Georgia from the South :
and, having captured Sunbury, — a seaport of
considerable wealth and importance, — he was
ordered to move upon Savannah. Colonel Archibald Campbell, sailing with a formidable force
from New York, was to supplement this demonstration by a direct attack upon the commercial
metropolis of Georgia. Thus caught between
the upper and the nether millstone, it was be-

ing upon the Continental establishment. It could scarcely, in
all fairness, have been addressed to the militia and the naval
forces.

lieved that Georgia would speedily and surely be ground down into absolute submission to British dominion. The two detachments sent forward by General Prevost, — one by sea, conducted by Lieutenant-Colonel Fuser, and ordered to reduce Sunbury, the other led by Lieutenant-Colonel Mark Prevost, penetrating by land and commissioned to devastate the lower portions of Georgia, — after forming a junction at Sunbury, were directed to take the town of Savannah in reverse, thus coöperating with Colonel Campbell who was expected at the same time to attack from the north. Through a want of concert in action these Florida columns failed of their objective. Opposed by Colonels Baker and White and by General James Screven, and resisted by Lieutenant-Colonel John McIntosh, commanding Fort Morris at Sunbury, — all acting under the orders of Colonel Elbert, who had taken post at the Great Ogeechee crossing and fortified that position with the intention of delivering battle there if the enemy succeeded in penetrating so far, — Prevost and Fuser, failing to effect the contemplated junction, abandoned the siege of Sunbury, and, retreating upon Florida, did not unite with Campbell in his attack upon Savannah.

By the 27th of December, 1778, the fleet transporting the expeditionary force under the command of that capable officer had crossed the bar and lay at anchor near the mouth of the Savannah River. General Howe hastily concentrated all his available forces for the defense of the capital of Georgia. At day-break, on the morning of the 29th, the first division of the British army — composed of all the light infantry, the New York volunteers, and the first battalion of the 71st regiment, and led by Lieutenant-Colonel Maitland — effected a landing in front of Girardeau's plantation. Thence a narrow causeway, about eight hundred yards long and with a ditch on each side, led through the swamp and rice-fields to Girardeau's residence, which stood upon a bluff some thirty feet above the level of the river delta. Rushing forward the enemy quickly succeeded in dislodging the small American party, under Captain Smith, which had been detailed to hold this position, and scaling the bluff gained possession of the high ground. This accomplished, the approach to Savannah was facile. Ignoring the strategic importance of this locality, and disregarding the earnest entreaty of Colonel Elbert that Brewton Hill — or Girardeau's Bluff as it was then called — should be fortified and defended to the last extremity, General Howe contented himself with posting only forty men there, and, disposing his army in the vicinity of Savannah, awaited the advance of Colonel Campbell. The British outnumbered the American forces. General Howe

formed his line of battle across the road leading
from Brewton Hill and Thunderbolt to Savannah, at a point about eight hundred yards distant from the gate opening into Governor
Wright's plantation. One brigade — consisting
chiefly of the regiments of Colonels Huger and
Thompson, and commanded by the former —
was stationed on the right. The other brigade
— composed of portions of the first, second,
third, and fourth battalions of Georgia Conti-
nentals, and under the command of Colonel Elbert — was posted on the left, its right resting
upon the road and its left extending to the rice-
fields of Governor Wright. Behind the left
wing of this brigade was the fort on the Savannah River bluff. The town of Savannah, en-
circling which were the remains of an old and
abandoned line of intrenchments, was in the rear
of the army. A few field-pieces were disposed
at advantageous points. Although informed by
Colonel George Walton, who, with one hundred
Georgia militia, was posted on the South Common behind the right of the American line, that
there was a private way through the swamp, by
means of which the enemy could pass from the
high grounds adjacent to Brewton Hill and gain
his rear, and although urged by him to have this
approach properly guarded, General Howe neg-
lected to attend to the matter, and thus committed another fatal error in the conduct of this
important affair.

No position more apt for defense could have been selected in the entire neighborhood than the bluff at Girardeau's plantation.[1] A regiment there embodied, with a few pieces of field artillery advantageously distributed along the brow, would have utterly shattered the advancing column of the enemy moving along a narrow rice-dam nearly half a mile in length, and with marish and impracticable grounds on either hand. The disparity between the contending forces rendered it all the more obligatory upon the American general to have taken advantage of this locality. It was the key to Savannah. Repulsed from this landing place, and defeated in the effort to obtain a base of operations here, the acquisition of Savannah would have proved to Colonel Campbell a difficult problem. Colonel Elbert realized this fact, and pressed it upon the attention of General Howe. He offered with his command to hold Girardeau's bluff against all comers. We marvel at the apathy and the negligence exhibited by the commander of the American forces.

It lies not within the compass of this hour to recount the incidents of an engagement which quickly culminated in the capture of the capital

[1] Judge Charlton, in his *Life of Major-General James Jackson*, p. 13, Augusta, Georgia, 1809, says: "The eye of a military man would at once have seen the importance of the Hill at the extremity of the causeway: it was the Thermopylæ of Savannah."

of Georgia, the loss of valuable stores, and the defeat of the Revolutionists. Attacked in front and rear the patriots soon gave way. When the retreat was sounded a panic ensued, and the Americans fled as best they could, and in a confused manner, through the town. Before the retiring army gained the head of the causeway over Musgrove's swamp,[1] west of Savannah, — the only pass by which a retreat was practicable, — the enemy secured a position to interrupt the crossing. By extraordinary exertions Colonel Roberts kept the British in check until the centre of the army made its escape. The American right flank, being between two fires, suffered severely. The Georgia militia, under Colonel Walton, who, shot through the thigh, fell from his horse and was made a prisoner, were wholly killed, wounded, or captured. The left, under the command of Colonel Elbert, continued the conflict with such pertinacity and gallantry that a retreat by the causeway became impracticable. That officer, therefore, attempted to lead his troops through the rice-fields lying between the Springfield causeway and the Savannah River. In doing so he encountered a heavy fire from

---

[1] This swamp, at a later date constituting a part of the Springfield plantation, and now so thoroughly drained, was then boggy, filled with brambles, and an almost impenetrable morass. It was here, on the morning of the 9th of October, 1779, that the assaulting columns, led by Count D'Estaing, encountered insuperable obstacles and frightful loss.

the enemy who had taken possession of the cause-way and of the adjacent high grounds of Ewens-burg. Reaching Musgrove Creek, Colonel El-bert found it filled with water, for the tide was high. Consequently, only those of his com-mand who could swim succeeded in crossing; and this they did with the loss of their arms and accoutrements. The others were either drowned or captured. Being an expert swimmer, Colonel Elbert made his escape, and retreated with the remnant of the army into South Carolina. Southern Georgia, bereft of her defenders, was quickly overrun by the enemy, who exacted trib-ute the most stringent.

Sunbury having fallen, and his arrangements for the occupation of all important posts along the right bank of the lower Savannah having been completed, Colonel Campbell resolved to push a column into the interior and finish the subjugation of the State by the capture of Au-gusta and the intimidation of the adjacent re-gion. In his advance he was confronted by Colo-nels Elbert, John Twiggs, and Benjamin and William Few. They were not strong enough, however, to defend the crossing at Brier Creek. Disappointed in the assistance which they ex-pected to receive from Colonels Williamson and Clarke, they retired slowly, skirmishing with Colonel Campbell's column as it moved upon Augusta. Upon its appearance before that town,

the Americans there posted retreated across the
Savannah River, and Augusta, without a struggle,
passed into the possession of the king's troops.
This advanced position Colonel Campbell did
not deem it prudent to hold, except for a little
while. Warned by the rapidly increasing forces
which General Benjamin Lincoln, newly arrived,
was concentrating at Purrysburg and Black
Swamp, he concluded to retire upon Ebenezer
and Savannah. During this retrograde movement he was pursued by General John Ashe,
with twenty-three hundred men, as far as Brier
Creek. There this North Carolina general halted,
and encamped in the angle formed by that
stream and the Savannah River. With this command Colonel Elbert was present.

At a council of war convened by General
Lincoln at General Rutherford's headquarters
at Williamson's plantation in Black Swamp, on
the 1st of March, 1779, it was resolved that all
available troops should be rapidly concentrated
at General Ashe's camp, preparatory to an early
and onward march for the recovery of Georgia.
That officer announced his position as secure,
and stated that his only need was a detachment
of artillerists with one or two field-pieces. This
want was recognized by General Lincoln, who
ordered Major Grimké, with two light guns and
a requisite number of cannoneers, to proceed to
his assistance.

Advised of General Lincoln's intentions, Colonel Campbell determined by a quick and unexpected blow to defeat the contemplated concentration of the American forces, and to frustrate this plan for circumscribing the king's troops in their occupation of Georgia soil. He resolved at once to dislodge General Ashe. Major McPherson, with the first battalion of the 71st regiment, some irregulars, and two field-pieces, and Lieutenant-Colonel Prevost, with the second battalion of the same regiment, Sir James Baird's corps of light infantry, three grenadier companies of the 60th regiment, Captain Tawes' troop of light dragoons, and about one hundred and fifty men of the Florida rangers and militia, were detailed for this service. Well did they perform the duty to which they were assigned. The command of General Ashe had been so much reduced by details that on the day of the engagement it did not exceed eight hundred men present for duty. Many of these were poorly armed and inadequately supplied with ammunition. The lack of circumspection and the want of preparation which characterized the conduct of the commander of the Americans on this occasion excite our surprise and merit severe criticism. The enemy had reached his vicinity before he was assured of any hostile approach. Hastily forming line of battle in three divisions, — the right under Colonel Young, the

centre under General Bryant, and the left, consisting of sixty Continental troops, one hundred
and fifty Georgia militia, and a field-piece,
under the command of Colonel Elbert assisted
by Lieutenant-Colonel John McIntosh and Major
John Habersham, — General Ashe advanced to
a position about a quarter of a mile in front of
his encampment and there awaited the enemy's
attack. His left rested upon Brier Creek, and
his right extended to within eight hundred yards
of the Savannah River swamp. When within
one hundred and fifty yards of the Americans,
and at four o'clock in the afternoon, Colonel
Prevost opened the engagement with his artillery
and pressed forward. Ashe's centre, which was
thrown a little in advance, did not withstand the
shock even for a few moments. It broke and
fled in wild confusion. The right also, so soon
as it was pressed, followed suit. The left alone
remained, and, under the valorous leadership of
Colonel Elbert, fought so stubbornly that Prevost found it necessary to order up his reserves
to support his right, which was confronted by this
small but gallant body. Notwithstanding the
great disparity in the numbers engaged, Elbert
prolonged the conflict until nearly every man of
his command was either killed, wounded, or captured. The fugitives from the American centre
and right sought shelter in the deep swamp bor-
dering upon the Savannah River. Such of them

as escaped the pursuit of the enemy and could swim, crossed to the Carolina shore. Many were drowned in the attempt. Colonel Elbert, — whom Colonel Prevost in his report designates as one of the best officers in the rebel army, — twenty-seven other officers, and two hundred privates were taken prisoners. One hundred and fifty Americans were killed upon the field and in the adjacent swamps, exclusive of such as were drowned in attempting to save themselves from slaughter by plunging into a deep and rapid river. Seven pieces of field artillery, a considerable quantity of ammunition, provisions, and baggage, and one thousand small arms fell into the hands of the victors. The multitude slain would seemingly claim credence for the report that in their pursuit of the fugitive Americans Sir James Baird cried aloud to his light infantry: "Every man of you that takes a prisoner shall lose his ration of rum." When overtaken in the Savannah River swamp, not a few of the militia were cruelly bayoneted by the exultant British soldiery.

Never was encampment more injudiciously located or more insecurely guarded. Never was command held in worse plight for action. The only ray of light, amid the gloom of the whole affair, was shed by the gallantry of Colonel Elbert and his followers. This defeat at Brier Creek disconcerted General Lincoln's plans and, in connection with General Howe's misfortune at Savannah, materially prolonged the struggle in this department. The tradition lives that Colonel Elbert, even when surrounded by the enemy, continued to offer the stoutest resistance. Finally he was struck down. A soldier was on the point of dispatching him with uplifted bayonet, when he gave the Masonic sign of distress. It was perceived by an officer, who intervened just in time to save the life of the brave Colonel.

Doctor Joseph Johnson [1] says that while a prisoner in the British camp Colonel Elbert was treated with great respect and kindness. Offers of promotion, honors, and rewards were extended, and persuasions used to seduce him from the American cause. His patriotism was proof against them all. These allurements having been repeatedly declined, an attempt was made, through the intervention of two Indians, to take his life. In his mercantile transactions Colonel Elbert had dealt largely with the Creeks and Cherokees, and his personal acquaintance with them was by no means limited. As the captain of a grenadier company, during Governor Wright's administration, he had escorted a deputation of chiefs to their homes in the Creek country. Discovering the purpose of the savages, he gave a signal which he had formerly used

---

[1] *Traditions and Reminiscences, chiefly of the American Revolution in the South,* etc., p. 475. Charleston. 1851.

among them. They recognized it at once, and, lowering their guns, the hired assassins came forward and extended their hands in token of amity. This dastardly attempt is not chargeable to the officers of the British army. From them Colonel Elbert, during his captivity, was the recipient only of courtesy and manly consideration. It is believed that it was suggested by lawless marauders and loyalists infesting the region, in the punishment of whose acts of atrocity Colonel Elbert had been most active.[1]

When he was exchanged in June, 1781, so thoroughly was his former command dispersed, and so completely were Georgia and South Carolina under the control of the enemy, that he waited upon the commander-in-chief and tendered his services. They were accepted by General Washington, who assigned him to duty. At the siege of Yorktown he was entrusted with the command of " the grand deposit of arms and military stores, a post of great trust and honor." Here, as elsewhere, he merited and received the commendation of all. With General

---

[1] During the siege of Savannah in September and October, 1779, as we learn from a letter written by Colonel Joseph Habersham, dated " Col Wylly's Tent near Savannah, 28th September 1779," and now in the possession of William Neyle Habersham, Esqr., Colonel Elbert was held a captive within the British lines. Painful must have been his emotions, finding himself still a prisoner, and incapable of uniting with his compatriots in the brave effort to liberate his home from British dominion.

Lafayette he contracted a firm friendship. One
of his sons he named in compliment to the distinguished marquis. Colonel Elbert continued
in the military service of the United Colonies
until the close of the Revolutionary War. He
was, as we have seen, appointed to a Lieutenant-
Colonelcy in February, 1776. On the 16th of
September in the same year he was advanced to
the grade of Colonel in the Continental army;
and on the 3d of November, 1783, he received
his commission as Brigadier-General. Subsequently he was complimented by the State of
Georgia with the position of Major-General of
militia.

When, upon the conclusion of peace, the
patriot army was disbanded, General Elbert returned to Savannah and resumed his commercial
pursuits. In July, 1785, by an almost unani-
mous vote, he was elected Governor of Georgia.
In the discharge of the duties of this high station
he manifested the same ability, energy, diligence,
good judgment, decision of character, and ex-
alted manhood which had characterized him in
other positions. Between the rivers Satilla and
St. Mary a band of freebooters had established
themselves. There they accumulated negroes,
horses, and cattle which they had stolen from
the honest and patriotic citizens of Georgia.
They were a pest to the neighborhood, defied
the laws, and plundered the adjacent territory.

One of the first official acts of Governor Elbert was to commission Colonel John Baker, with a sufficient force, to capture and disperse these villains, and restore the property in their possession to its rightful owners. His efforts were also directed to the pacification of the Indians who, on the northern confines of the State, "incited by disaffected and mercenary persons," were committing depredations and disturbing the peace of the region.

In acknowledgment of the universal respect and gratitude for his meritorious services to the youthful commonwealth and in the cause of American freedom during the Revolutionary War, the General Assembly of Georgia complimented Count D'Estaing with a grant of twenty thousand acres of land, and invested him with "all the privileges, liberties, and immunities of a free citizen of the State." It was the pleasing duty of Governor Elbert, through Commissioner John McQueen, to communicate to the Count this expression of the public esteem. In returning his thanks, this illustrious Frenchman said : "The mark of its satisfaction which the State of Georgia was pleased to give me after I had been wounded, was the most healing balm that could have been applied to my pains whenever they were most acute. Nothing could be more flattering than to be admitted as a proprietor in a State that has so much distinguished itself in supporting the common cause." It was his avowed purpose, with a portion of the proceeds of the sale of these lands, to erect, at the entrance of Paris, a monument "to the States," commemorative of "the glory of the King and of those patriots who contributed to the epoch of liberty." The distractions in France which quickly supervened, his engagements as vice-admiral of the navy, and his tragic fate prevented the consummation of this memorable intention. The gubernatorial career of General Elbert was honorable and prosperous.

Several times did he act as the representative of the State of Georgia in accommodating difficulties and negotiating treaties with the Creek and Cherokee Indians. Among the latter, that concluded at the Augusta Convention, held on the 31st of May, 1783, in which Georgia was represented by Governor Lyman Hall, General John Twiggs, Colonel Elijah Clarke, Colonel William Few, the Honorable Edward Telfair, and General Samuel Elbert, will be specially remembered. On that occasion eighteen of the leading chiefs and head warriors of the Cherokees were present. General Elbert's acquaintance with the Indian nations was, as we have seen, extensive, and his influence over them quite marked. Alexander McGillivray was at one time a clerk in his counting-house.

Secure in the esteem and accompanied by the

gratitude of his fellow-citizens, upon the expira-
tion of his term of office as Governor of Georgia
General Elbert was elected Sheriff of the county
of Chatham.[1] Of this lucrative and responsible
position was he the incumbent when overtaken
by death at the early age of forty-eight years.
As a soldier he was brave, active, and intelli-
gent. Among his companions he was known as
a dashing officer and a hard fighter. Never did
he abandon a field which could be held by stub-
born valor. Gentlemanly in deportment, handsome in person, erect and graceful in carriage,
and gallant in bearing, he was magnetic in his
intercourse and commanding in his influence.
His social qualities were of an attractive character, and his intellectual and moral endowments of
a high order. For military affairs he possessed
a natural fondness and manifested uncommon
aptitude. His reputation was above reproach.
His benevolence was large, and his impulses were
open, generous, patriotic, chivalrous, and noble.
He was one of those excellent and good men
who, in the language of Emerson, "make the
earth wholesome." By the entire community
was his demise sincerely mourned, and the General Assembly of Georgia, in acknowledgment of

[1] The office of Sheriff was at this time esteemed of prime dignity and moment. The tradition, inherited from the mother
country, that the High Sheriff should be the best man of his
county, had not then been either forgotten or ignored in the youthful commonwealth.

his valuable public services and in perpetuation of his good fame, named in his honor one of the most fertile counties within the limits of this commonwealth. We conclude this sketch by reproducing from the "Georgia Gazette" the following contemporaneous notice of his death and burial : —

"Died last Saturday,[1] after a lingering sickness, aged 48 years, SAMUEL ELBERT, *Major General* of the Militia of this State, *Vice President* of the Society of Cincinnati, and *Sheriff* of the County of Chatham. His death was announced by the discharge of minute guns, and the colours of Fort Wayne and the vessels in the harbour being displayed half-mast high. An early and warm attachment to the cause of his country stimulated him to exert those natural talents he possessed for a military life throughout the late glorious and successful contest with ability and general approbation, for which he was promoted to the rank of *Brigadier General* in the *Army of the United States.*

"In the year 1785, his country chose him, by their general suffrage, Governor and Commander-in-Chief of the State, which office he executed with fidelity, and discharged its various duties with becoming attention and dignity. The appointments of Major General of the Militia, and Sheriff of this County, were further marks of

[1] November 1, 1788.

the confidence of his country, whose interests
he had always at heart, and whose appointments
he received and executed with a grateful re-
membrance that his conduct through life had
met the approbation of his fellow citizens. In
private life he was among the first to promote
useful and benevolent societies. As a Chris-
tian he bore his painful illness with patience
and firmness, and looked forward to his great
change with an awful and fixed hope of future
happiness. As a most affectionate husband and
parent, his widow and six children have great
cause to lament his end, and society in general
to regret the loss of a valuable member. His
remains were attended on Sunday to Christ
Church by the Ancient Society of Masons [of
which he was the *Past Grand Master* in this
State], with the members of the Cincinnati as
mourners, accompanied by a great number of
his fellow citizens whom the Rev: Mr Lindsay
addressed in a short but well adapted discourse on
the solemn occasion. Minute guns were fired
during the funeral, and every other honour was
paid his memory by a respectable military pro-
cession composed of the Artillery and other
Militia Companies. The body was afterwards
deposited at the family burial place on the
Mount at Rae's Hall." [1]

---

[1] *The Georgia Gazette,* No. 302. Savannah, Georgia. November 6, 1788.

The Indian grave-mound near the confluence of Pipe-Maker's Creek and the Savannah River, which a later generation appropriated as a convenient place for modern sepulture, still stands, marking the spot where, nearly a century agone, the dust of a General in the army of the Revolution, of an honored citizen, and of a Governor of this commonwealth mingled with the ashes of the ancestors of the venerable Tomo-chi-chi. Although Rae's Hall has passed into the ownership of strangers, — although his memorial stone has fallen, — although soulless brambles and envious forest trees have obliterated all traces of the inhumation, — the name of Samuel Elbert is enshrined in the annals of Georgia, and his memory will be cherished by all who are not unmindful of the lessons inculcated by a life of virtue, of valor, of probity, of benevolence, of patriotism, and of fidelity to trust reposed.

Thus, my friends of the Georgia Historical Society, reviving these memories as they have been gleaned amid the lights and shadows of a remote and heroic past, and grouping them into a tribute expressive of our grateful appreciation of uncommon virtue and excellence, we offer this memorial of one who deserves high place in this Hall[1] dedicated to the perpetuation of

[1] The address was delivered in Hodgson Hall, the home of the Georgia Historical Society.

characters and events memorable in the history of this colony and commonwealth. Due preservation of and suitable meditation upon such recollections constitute no mean part of your mission, which, if worthily pursued, will enure to the general good, and encourage in the present a generous emulation of whatever dignified and ennobled the days that are gone.

> " There is a history in all men's lives,
> Figuring the nature of the times deceas'd ;
> The which observ'd a man may prophesy,
> With a near aim, of the main chance of things
> As yet not come to life, which in their seeds,
> And weak beginnings lie intreasured.
> Such things become the hatch and brood of time."

Charles. C. Jones. Jr.

Augusta, Georgia, *December* 4, 1886.

SUPPLEMENTAL NOTES.

I.

THE white population of Georgia, at the inception of the war of the Revolution, did not probably exceed twenty thousand, of all ages. Governor Wright,[1] on the 20th of December, 1773, reported to the Earl of Dartmouth that there were then inhabiting the province eighteen thousand whites and fifteen thousand blacks. During the continuance of the struggle Georgia contributed to the Continental army two thousand six hundred and seventy-nine men. Such, at least, is the best information which can be obtained.[2]

With regard to the militia, called from time to time into the field, Major-General James Jackson, who, in subordinate capacities and as a major and lieutenant-colonel, was an active participant in the entire contest, furnishes this estimate. He says that during the year 1775, and until the spring of 1776, Georgia had one thousand militiamen in service. For the years 1776 and 1777 he computes the militia in active service at seven hundred and fifty, exclusive of two battalions of minutemen of seven hundred and fifty each, a state regiment of horse two hundred and fifty strong, and three additional troops of forty men each, under the command of a major. In 1778, besides the state corps, two thousand militiamen were in the field for nearly six months. During the years 1779, 1780, 1781, and 1782

---

[1] P. R. O. Am. & W. Ind., No. 235.

[2] Lossing's *Pictorial Field-Book of the Revolution*, vol. ii. p. 631. New York. 1859.

he estimates the militia constantly in service at seven hundred and fifty men. Among these was not included his own Legion, formed by order of General Greene in 1781. When to these we add many partisans never borne upon the rolls of either the Continental or the State establishment, and who depended almost exclusively upon their own resources and exertions for arms, munitions, and subsistence, it will readily be perceived that the entire manhood of the Republican element must, at some time or other, have been actively enlisted in the warlike effort to win the independence of the confederated States. Georgia — the youngest of the thirteen colonies — certainly contributed her full quota of men and resources in the achievement of American liberty.

II.

The following is a roster of the FIRST REGIMENT OF CHATHAM COUNTY MILITIA, when Samuel Elbert was Major-General of the State forces[1] : —

> James Jackson, *Colonel Commanding.*
> James Gunn, *Lieutenant-Colonel.*
> Benjamin Fishbourne, *Major.*
> Justus H. Scheuber, *Adjutant.*
> Jacob Waldburg, *Clerk of the Regiment.*

LIGHT DRAGOONS.

> *First Lieutenant,* Isaac Young.
> *Second Lieutenant,* David Sarzedas.
> *Cornet,* Isaac Lagardere.

ARTILLERY.

> *Captain,* Edward Lloyd.
> *First Lieutenant,* Thomas Elfe.
> *Second Lieutenant,* John Wanden.

[1] See MS. Order Book of Colonel James Jackson.

LIGHT INFANTRY.

Captain, Benjamin Lloyd.
First Lieutenant, Elisha Elon.
Second Lieutenant, Benjamin Butler

SAVANNAH.

Captain, Frederick Shick.
Lieutenant, Joseph Welscher.

SEA ISLANDS.

Captain, John Barnard.
First Lieutenant, Robert Barnard.
Second Lieutenant, Solomon Shad.

WHITE BLUFF.

Captain, Josiah Tattnall.
First Lieutenant, John King.
Second Lieutenant, Peter Theus.

LITTLE OGEECHEE.

Captain, David Rees.
First Lieutenant, Benjamin Wilson.
Second Lieutenant, James Martin Gibbons.

CHEROKEE HILL.

Captain, ―― ――.
First Lieutenant, Thomas Palmer.
Second Lieutenant, ―― ――.

GREAT OGEECHEE.

Captain, Robert Holmes.
First Lieutenant, Edmund Adams.
Second Lieutenant, Simons Maxwell.

The town of Savannah then constituted "one militia district," and Captain Shick was designated as its commanding officer. Although the war had ended, rude alarms were not infrequent. Indian tribes beyond the Alatamaha, and at other points on the confines of the white settlements, were restless and inclined to indulge in depredations and murders. Upon the evacuation of Savannah three hundred runaway slaves, who had been enlisted by the British during their occupancy of the town, refused to return to the service of their owners. Styling themselves the "King of England's soldiers," and attracting to their companionship the disaffected of their own color, they established themselves in the fastnesses of the swamps on both sides of the Savannah River, whence they sallied forth by night for plunder and butchery, to the disquietude and annoyance of the adjacent inhabitants. One of their fortified camps on Bear Creek, in Effingham County, was, in May, 1786, carried by the First Regiment of the Chatham County Militia, assisted by troops from Beaufort, South Carolina. Although many of the marauders were either killed or captured with arms in their hands, numbers escaped, who, concealing themselves in tangled brakes, continued, as opportunity occurred, their work of theft and violence. The period was, in many quarters, fraught with anxiety and apprehension. Fears were entertained of a servile insurrection. The office of a militiaman was then by no means a sinecure, and for several years after the cessation of hostilities between England and the United Colonies the duties of the companies composing the Chatham regiment were onerous. Gradually, however, domestic peace was confirmed. In the restoration of order and tranquillity the militia of Georgia rendered efficient service.

So great was the scarcity of powder in the possession of the military authorities in Savannah, that Colonel James Jackson, on the 22d of June, 1786, apologizes for an expenditure of one hundred pounds "at the funeral of that great and good man, General Greene." In his communication to the secretary of the Executive Council he inquires: "Will Council be so good as to let me know if they approve of my conduct, for I would rather pay for that powder myself than lay under a censure for it? It was thought here by all ranks of people the least that could be shown the remains of that hero by the State of Georgia."